AN ORCA
YOUNG
READER

Jesse's Star

Ellen Schwartz

ORCA BOOK PUBLISHERS

Canadian Cataloguing in Publication Data
Schwartz, Ellen, 1949–
Jesse's star

ISBN 1-55143-143-2

I. Title.
PS8587.C578J47 2000   jC813'.54   C00-910207-8   PZ7.S4074Je 2000

Library of Congress Catalog Card Number: 00-100931

Orca Book Publishers gratefully acknowledges the support of
our publishing programs provided by the following agencies:
the Department of Canadian Heritage, The Canada Council
for the Arts, and the British Columbia Arts Council.

Cover design by Christine Toller
Cover illustration by Don Kilby
Interior illustrations by Kirsti

IN CANADA	IN THE UNITED STATES
Orca Book Publishers	Orca Book Publishers
PO Box 5626, Station B	PO Box 468
Victoria, BC Canada	Custer, WA USA
V8R 6S4	98240-0468

02 01 00 • 5 4 3 2 1

For David

*The author would like to thank Mrs. Davies'
grade 3 – 4 class at Frank Hobbs
Elementary School, and Ann Featherstone,
for their editorial assistance.*

Chapter One

"Remember, children, your family reports are due tomorrow," Ms. Brannigan reminded the class as they headed out the door.

Jesse groaned.

That stupid assignment. He hadn't even started it yet.

What was he going to do?

Scowling, he shoved his hands in his

pockets and started across the school field.

Tomorrow? No way.

What a dumb project anyway. "Find out how your relatives came to Canada," Ms. Brannigan had said. "Find out when they came and why they came, and what the conditions were like in the country where they came from. Write it all up in a report. Then we'll put all the reports together in a big scrapbook that the whole class can share."

Yippee, Jesse thought, kicking a stone. As if he cared about his dumb old relatives. What difference did it make when they came to Canada, or why, or how? They were all dead now, had been dead for years. They got here and now Jesse's family lived here — that was all that mattered. So why bother going back in time to find out all that stuff?

Jesse whacked at a tree with a stick.

And how was he supposed to find it all out anyway? He knew nothing about his relatives, didn't remember hearing any stories. He had no papers or pictures or scrapbooks or diaries, like some of the other kids. And the stupid report was due tomorrow.

Jesse aimed a stone at a telephone pole. *Ping!*

Shoot. He'd have to ask his parents. And then they'd know he'd left it until the last minute. Again. Last time, with the science project, was bad enough. But now, again ...

Well, there was no help for it. No one else to ask. Might as well face the music — and hope his mom or dad could bail him out.

He entered the kitchen. No sign of his dad, but his mom was there, stuffing papers into her briefcase.

"Hey, Mom," he said, "how's it going?" No harm buttering her up a bit first.

"Hi, Jesse." She waved a hand as she hurriedly slipped on her dress shoes.

"Got a minute?"

"As a matter of fact, no. I've got to

dash. What's up?"

"Where're you going?"

"Big meeting at the office — remember?"

Jesse's heart sank. "But Mom, I need your help."

"For what?" she said, stuffing papers into her briefcase.

"A social studies report. About our relatives."

"Which relatives? What about them?"

"The long-ago ones. The ones who first came to Canada. I need to know when they came and why they came and how they came and —"

Jesse's mom laughed. "That's quite a project."

"I know, Mom, that's why I need to ask you —"

"Not now, that's for sure."

"But Mom —"

"Sorry, Jesse, I'm running late as it is. Tell you what. We'll sit down tomorrow after school. You can ask me all the questions you want. Promise." She ruffled his hair, then started putting on her jacket.

Panic set in. "But Mom, it's due tomorrow."

She stopped with the jacket halfway on. "It's what?"

Jesse lowered his eyes.

"You left this until the last minute?"

"Well, yeah, but —"

"Jesse!"

"Aw, Mom, you know how much I hate Social Studies, and it's a dumb assignment anyway —"

"That is no excuse."

"I know, but —"

"I can't believe you've done it again, Jesse. You've got to smarten up!"

"I know, Mom. I will. Really. But in the meantime can't you at least tell me when they came? And where they came from?"

She frowned at him, shaking her head. "They came from Russia. Around the end of the nineteenth century."

"*Around?*" Jesse repeated, dismayed. "Don't you even know the year?"

"Not the exact year."

"Why not?"

"Because nobody kept any records."

"Why not?"

His mom ran a brush through her hair. "They were poor Jews, Jesse. They escaped at a time when many Jews were leaving Russia. Things were crazy. People were dying. Everyone was in a hurry to get out. There was no time to keep proper records."

"Some help that is!" Jesse snapped.

"Look, young man, this is your own fault. If you hadn't let it slide —"

"OK, OK. But how did they come? Do you at least know that?"

The doorbell rang. His mom opened it. "Oh, hi, Sally," she said, ushering in the babysitter. "Just in time. Dinner's in the oven. I'll be back around nine." She grabbed her briefcase, gave Jesse a quick hug. "Be good."

"Mom!" Jesse wailed.

She turned back, giving him an exasperated look. "Try looking up in the attic. Your great-great-grandfather — Yossi Mendelsohn, his name was — was about your age when the family left Russia. There's an old traveling case that used to belong to him up there somewhere."

"What's in it?"

"I don't remember."

Jesse groaned.

"There might be some passports or diaries or other documents that can help you."

"Fat chance."

His mom gave him a sharp look. "Well, do you have any other ideas?"

"No," Jesse said miserably.

Her voice softened. "Go ahead, give it a try, Jesse. You never know what you might find."

Blowing him a kiss, she left.

Chapter Two

Jesse pushed aside the trap door and pulled himself up into the attic. A speck of dust tickled his nose. *Ahh-chooo!* Blech! It was dusty up here.

Smelled, too. Old and musty. Yuck. Jesse stood up.

Clunk! "Ouch!" Why hadn't Mom told him the attic walls were so steep?

Rubbing his head, he looked around.

Cartons, suitcases and trunks crammed the narrow space.

Great, he thought. He was going to die from the dust, if he didn't knock himself out first. And how on earth was he supposed to find that box in all this mess, anyway?

Grumbling to himself about how he'd rather be riding his bike or kicking around a soccer ball with the guys or practically anything else you could think of, Jesse started searching.

He pushed aside an old dresser to reach a box wedged under the eaves. Printing showed between the flaps. Maybe ...

No, just old, musty-smelling magazines, their pages stuck together.

Shoot.

Jesse opened another carton. Clothes, it looked like. He lifted out a pair of blue booties, then a tiny yellow sweater embroidered with bunnies. His baby clothes. Embarrassing! Good thing the guys weren't around.

He tore open another box. Several pairs of ancient ice skates, with worn toes and dull blades.

Fooey.

Maybe his mom was wrong, and that old box of Yossi's wasn't up here, and this whole thing was a waste of time. I'll give it five more minutes, he promised, and then that's it.

He searched the shelves of a bookcase, but found only toppled-over books.

OK, forget it. It wasn't his fault. He'd tried. He'd just have to tell Ms. Brannigan that he couldn't —

Turning, Jesse caught his foot on the corner of the bookcase. WHOMP! Down he fell.

Lying flat on the floor, he saw it. A box. Shoved under the bottom shelf of the bookcase. He pulled it out. Dark brown, heavy leather, with two cracked leather straps that buckled to hold it shut. Flat and rectangular, about the size of his mom's briefcase.

This must be the one. Yossi's traveling case. In spite of himself, a tingle went up Jesse's back.

The straps were stiff with age. One metal buckle opened easily, but the other was rusted shut. Jesse pried. He shoved. He wiggled. Rust flaked off on his fingers. Finally, he managed to shove the prong out of the hole. Freed, the strap slid through the buckle.

Get ready for nothing, Jesse told himself. Still, as he lifted the lid, he felt strangely excited.

An old photograph. A blue cloth bag tied with a yellow drawstring.

That was all.

Shoot! Nothing good. Nothing to help him.

He knew it.

Now what?

Give up. Go downstairs.

Thanks a lot, Yossi, he thought. Some help you are.

Jesse started to close the box, but

something made him take out the photograph. It must have originally been black and white, but now it was yellowish brown and curled at the edges. He peered at it. A group of people, forty or so, were standing in front of a large ship, most clutching small canvas bags. They looked tired. And poor. Their clothes were shabby and plain. The men and boys wore cloth caps; the women wore scarves. At the front of the group stood a boy about Jesse's age, nine or ten. Short pants held up by suspenders, white shirt not quite tucked in, knee socks disappearing into high-buttoned boots, short-brimmed cap shoved over dark curls.

All the people looked serious. Proud, sort of, Jesse thought. Determined. But not smiling. They looked like people who didn't smile much.

Except for the boy. A big grin lit his face.

Jesse wondered if this was Yossi. A tingle on the back of his neck told him it was. He turned the photo over, searching for names. There were none, but in faded, now-brown ink, was written the words: "Canada! 1890."

Not just "Canada," but Canada with an exclamation point. These people were really glad to be here. It meant a lot to them — more than he'd realized. And at least now he knew his relatives had come in 1890. That was better than nothing.

But not much. One little fact wasn't going to save his report. If only there was a diary in the box, or passports, or —

Then he remembered the cloth bag. He opened the drawstring. Something inside glittered. Jesse shook it into his hand. Out fell a tarnished, six-sided Star of David on a slender chain.

Big deal, Jesse thought. What's so special about an old Jewish star?

But he took a closer look, and saw gold glinting out from under the dull brown tarnish. And was he imagining it, or did his palm feel warm where the star lay? No, that couldn't be.

Idly, Jesse unclasped the chain and fastened it around his neck. The star rested in the hollow of his throat. Heat seemed to melt into his chest, right where the star touched his skin. He grasped the star in his hand.

Jesse began to feel dizzy. The air in the attic went blurry, as if he'd put on a pair of glasses coated with oil. The bookcase shimmered in front of his eyes, then melted away. The box in his hands grew lighter, then disappeared. Jesse felt his hair grow longer. He felt his jeans shrink into knee-length trousers, his high-tops turn into heavy boots.

A tumble-down wooden hut hovered blurrily in front of him. An apple tree materialized hazily. Everything — his clothes, the hut, the tree — was in black and white, with yellowed tones. The musty smell of dust and old books faded away, and a whiff of hay and apples and barnyard floated on the air.

Somehow, Jesse knew he was turning

into Yossi. He was becoming his great-great-grandfather! Thoughts started coming into his head in a new language. At once he realized it was Yiddish. Yet, strangely, he understood it perfectly, and Russian, too. And instead of being odd or frightening, it all felt right. Normal. As if this was the way things were supposed to be.

Like a camera coming into focus, the blurriness began to clear. The smells became sharper. The dizziness went away. Black and white transformed into bright, vivid color.

It was autumn, 1890, in the small Russian village of Braslav. And Jesse was Yossi.

Chapter Three

"Look at me!" Yossi yelled, teetering on the garden path. This was the longest he'd ever managed to stay up on his stilts. One second ... two ... three ... "Quick, everybody, look!" Six ... seven ...

He was as high as the branches of the apple tree, so close he could reach out and grab a ripe red apple — only he didn't dare let go of his stilts, not even for a

second, because he was still learning.

"Miriam, Mama, Papa, look!"

Miriam, clipping bunches of dill weed in Mama's herb garden, looked. Papa, his axe poised over the wood chopping block, looked. Mama, up to her elbows in a bucket of soapy water, looked.

"Yossi Mendelsohn," Mama hollered, shaking a soapy fist, "you are supposed to be picking apples, not prancing around like a clown."

Papa's two black eyebrows drew together in one angry line. "Put away those ridiculous stilts this minute! Whoever heard of such a thing, hobbling around up in the clouds? There's work to be done."

"But Mama, Papa, look at me! I've never stayed up so long." Twelve seconds, thirteen … Yossi teetered, then righted himself. "See how I'm improving? Yesterday I could only stay up half this long. Soon I'll be able to pick the apples without even using a ladder!"

"We are not waiting until that fortunate day comes," Papa said threateningly. "You'll pick those apples *now, with* a ladder."

"*And* without dropping them all in the mud, like usual," Mama added, going into the cottage to fetch more dirty clothes.

"One more minute," Yossi begged. "Just one. For luck. Then, I promise, I'll pick every apple. I won't miss a single one."

"Yossi —" Papa scolded, but Yossi teetered away, pretending not to hear. He so desperately wanted to be good on the stilts. "Silly Yossi." "Clumsy Yossi." That's what all the villagers called him. And Yossi couldn't blame them. He was forever dropping things. Or bashing into people. Or tripping over his own feet. Even just walking the village cow to pasture, he managed to fall into a puddle or get the cow stuck in a swamp.

But then he had discovered the stilts. Simon, the village carpenter, had carved him a pair. And now Yossi was determined to master the stilts. What fun it was to soar so high above the heads of all the villagers! How powerful he felt! Best of all, if he could only become expert at stilt-walking, everyone would stop laughing at him. Stop teasing him. Stop calling him names.

And just look how well he was doing! One foot, the other foot ... past the herb garden where Miriam knelt beside her basket ... Left, right ... past the chopping block where Papa balanced a round of fir ... Step, step ... over to where Mama's two laundry buckets sat, one with soapy water, for scrubbing the clothes, the other with clear water, for rinsing ...

Forward, march ... Yossi's excitement mounted. This was his best yet. He'd taken so many steps, he'd lost count already. How skillful he was! How acrobatic —

Mama stepped out of the cottage, her arms full of clothes. The motion caught Yossi's eye. He turned. He leaned. "Woah —" Farther. "Wooaahh —" He tried to push himself back the other way. He succeeded. He was upright — but only for a second. Then he began to tip the other way. "Wah — woo — wow — woaahhh —"

One stilt landed in the bucket of sudsy water. The bucket tipped. The soapy clothes spilled onto the ground.

"Yossi!" Mama yelled.

"Waaaahhhh —" Frantically, Yossi stabbed the other stilt to the side. It landed in the other bucket. With a whoosh, the clean clothes splashed onto the dirt.

"WOOOAAAHHHOOOAAAHHH!!" Yossi landed on top of the clothes.

"I'll kill him, so help me God!" Mama hollered, advancing on Yossi. "His neck I'll strangle!"

"I'll assist you," Papa roared. "With pleasure!"

"Oh, Yossi," Miriam said with a sympathetic sigh.

"I'm sorry, Mama," Yossi said. He tried to get up but his feet slipped on the soapy puddle. "I'll fix it. I'll clean it. I'll wash the clothes." Dripping, he managed to stand.

Mama and Papa stood glaring at him. Please God, Yossi thought, don't let them take away my stilts.

"You were supposed to be picking the apples," Papa began.

"Yes, Papa."

"Lord knows, we have to get the crop picked and put away before the thieving Russian soldiers come to steal it out from under our noses!"

"Yes, Papa."

"So what are you doing, playing with those foolish sticks, prancing in the air, making enough trouble for ten rascally boys? Is that helpful?"

"Yes, Papa. I mean, no, Papa."

Now Mama spoke. "You will put the stilts away."

"Yes, Mama." Thank you, God, he thought.

"You will fetch me fresh water. Two buckets full."

"Yes, Mama."

"You will wash the clothes."

"Yes, Mama." He gulped. He'd only

offered to do that to make Mama stop yelling. He hadn't thought she'd really make him do it.

"Then you will pick the apples."

"Yes, Papa."

"AND YOU WILL STAY OUT OF TROUBLE FOR THE REST OF THE DAY!" Mama and Papa shouted together.

"Yes, Mama. Yes, Papa."

"Now, go."

Yossi scooped up the stilts. His wet trousers clung to him, and water sloshed in his boots. As he passed the herb garden, Miriam hissed. "Psst, Yossi!"

He turned.

Miriam winked. "I'll help you."

Yossi winked back. "Thanks."

No mystery why Miriam was being so nice. It was because he'd done her a favor the day before. Miriam was fourteen, old enough to wed, and yesterday Golda, the matchmaker, had come to the cottage to announce that she'd picked Miriam a husband. Jonah. Jonah with the watery eyes. Jonah with the clammy hands.

Yossi knew Miriam didn't like Jonah. And he knew something else, too. That she was sweet on Daniel, son of their neighbor Sadie.

So Yossi had done some fast thinking. He'd pointed out that Jonah was left-handed, and Miriam was right-handed, and when they stood side by side under the *chuppah*, the bridal canopy, and reached for the ritual cup of wine they both would drink from, they'd bump hands and spill the wine. What a bad omen that would be!

"*Oy*, a very bad omen," Golda had agreed worriedly, and Miriam's eyes had twinkled.

Then, slyly, Yossi had mentioned that Daniel was right-handed. And before you knew it, Golda was suggesting, just as if she'd thought of it herself, that Daniel would be a perfect match for Miriam. So it was decided.

Later, Miriam had given Yossi a big hug.

Now, Yossi lifted the two wooden buckets

and headed to the well. With Miriam's help he could finish all his chores in time to fit in one more practice session on the stilts before the evening meal. And he had to practice. So he would improve. So he could show the rest of the village that Yossi Mendelsohn was someone to be respected. Not jeered at.

Chapter Four

The next morning, Yossi grabbed both handles of a large straw basket and lifted. "Unnhh!" Loaded to the brim with beets, the basket was heavy. His thin arms ached.

But he didn't complain. He'd show everyone he could work like a grown-up. And, he told himself, all this lifting and carrying would make him stronger for stilt-walking.

Each family in Braslav tended a small kitchen garden of its own, for herbs and fresh greens. But together they tilled a communal plot, where they grew crops for all. Today, they were starting the autumn harvest with the beets. In a few days, the potatoes. Last, the turnips. And then the root cellar — an earth-walled building dug into the ground next to the garden — would be brimming with the hearty vegetables that, God willing, would keep them alive during the long, cold winter.

Even the *Rebbe*, the religious leader of the village, rolled up the sleeves of his long black robe, and toiled like a common worker. In a small village like Braslav, everyone had to pitch in.

Yossi lugged the basket toward a large wooden barrel that stood between the garden and the root cellar. Almost there ... almost ... THERE! Now all he had to do was lift up the basket and dump his load into the barrel.

Earlier in the day, it hadn't been so

hard. That was when Yossi's arms weren't so tired. But now they ached with fatigue. He could have sworn that the beets grew heavier, and the sides of the barrel rose higher, as the day wore on.

He took a deep breath. Up, he heaved. Knee-high. Waist-high. Chest-high. Shoulder — ahhh — ohhh — NOOO! — The beets shifted. The basket overturned, spilling its load on Golda, the matchmaker, who had just come to unload a basket of her own.

"Owww!" Golda yelled, hopping on one foot. "My toe! My foot! I'm injured!"

Yossi heard a giggle. He turned. Miriam's hand was clamped over her mouth. She winked at him.

Yossi grinned. It *was* funny, the sight of Golda hopping around like a crazed chicken.

But right now, the look in Golda's eye wasn't one bit funny.

Yossi began to put the basket over his head. Too late. Golda had spotted him.

"You! Yossi Mendelsohn! You clumsy oaf! You beet-spilling trouble-maker!"

"I'm sorry, Golda, I didn't mean to —" Yossi began, but Mama and Papa came running. They scolded Yossi, then hustled Golda away, murmuring apologies.

Yossi sighed. He'd done it again. Why did accidents always happen to him? How he longed to help with the beets, to make himself useful, to show what a fine boy he was.

"Clumsy child …," he heard someone say. "Always underfoot …," someone else grumbled.

Just wait, Yossi thought, as he sheepishly began picking up the spilled beets. Just wait until I master the stilts. Then you'll see.

Finally, all the beets were dug. Mud-bespattered, leaning on their spades, the villagers gathered 'round to admire the harvest. The pile of beets curved above the edges of the barrel.

"Praise God," cried Mama.

"Such a bountiful crop," said Papa.

"Plenty for everyone," said Simon with a satisfied sigh.

"True, true, Simon," Sadie, Daniel's mother, put in, "we'll all have full bellies this winter."

Golda, now miraculously recovered, shoved importantly to the front. "I knew, friends, when we planted the seeds, that they were special. A good crop will come from these seeds, I said. I knew it in my bones. Some have a way of knowing these things."

"Oh, be quiet, you old busybody," Yossi said under his breath, and Miriam giggled.

The Rebbe came forward, his long black robe muddy. "Hurry, friends," he said. "We must get the crop safely stored in the root cellar before the soldiers make off with it."

Yossi groaned. He wanted nothing more than to rest, but he knew the Rebbe was right. Several years before, in 1881, Czar Alexander II had been killed, and many Russian people had blamed the Jews. Since then, Russian soldiers had run wild in the countryside, terrorizing Jewish villages. Innocent people had been killed, their homes burned to the ground. Thousands of Jews, the lucky ones, had escaped — to other countries in Europe, even across the sea to the New World.

Not so the Jews of Braslav. A troop of Russian soldiers had an encampment near the village, and they seemed to delight in tormenting the villagers. "Jewish devils," the soldiers called them, robbing and beating them at will. Yet, although they despised the Jews, they refused to let them go, keeping them prisoner in their own village.

Sometimes Yossi thought it was because the Jews were an easy source of food. Often, when the soldiers' supplies ran low, they helped themselves to the villagers' livestock and crops. Just last month they'd made off with Simon's flock of laying hens. When he tried to stop them, they burned down his carpenter shop. Yossi could still picture the leaping flames, fed by Simon's precious supply of wood.

So Yossi knew the Rebbe was right. So far, the soldiers hadn't discovered the root cellar. It was important to hide the beets before they came again.

Wearily, he took his place between Mama and Papa, loading boxes, a layer of beets, then a layer of straw, so the beets would stay fresh and moist all winter; then handing the full boxes down the line, ready to start filling the next.

"Faster, Yossi, in case the soldiers are nearby," Mama urged.

"What's new, they're always nearby," said Rivka, Simon's wife.

"But if the beets are hidden away in the root cellar —" Yossi began.

"What's to stop them from finding the root cellar and taking all the beets?" said

Eli, the potter — and the gloomiest man in Braslav.

"Just like they took my hens," said Simon.

"Be glad they spared your life, Simon," Golda said, wagging a finger.

"For not having his head hacked off he should be grateful?" Rivka said.

"That's what they did to old Sam Rubin in Vladstok, may he rest in peace," Golda said. "He refused to let them take his horse. Worthless old nag, but Sam loved the poor beast. They chopped off Sam's head, then set fire to his cottage."

Yossi shuddered.

"God deliver us from this tormented country," Sadie said.

"If only, Sadie, if only ...," Papa said, raising a hand to heaven.

"Hannah, Sam's widow, made it to Canada, they say," Golda added.

"Canada," Mama repeated. "I hear it's a marvelous place. Forests so big you could ride for days and never reach the end of them ..."

"Clear, fresh water ...," Papa added.

"And no Russian soldiers!" Simon shouted to the cheers of all.

Canada ... Canada ... Yossi rolled the name around on his tongue. It sounded wonderful. It sounded like freedom.

Eli laughed harshly. "And how would we get to Canada, friends? How can we ever get away from Braslav with those soldiers watching us all the time?"

"It's because they love us so," Sadie joked, and everyone laughed.

"Hah!" Eli said with a toss of his head. "It's only for the pleasure of finding new ways to torment us."

"They hate Jews, but they won't let us leave. Some sense that makes," Rivka said.

"Faster, faster!" The Rebbe came down the line of workers.

Yossi worked feverishly, loading box after box. Then, in the distance, he heard a sound.

Hoof beats.

So did the other villagers.

"They're coming!"

"Not again!"

"Spare us!"

The barrel was still over half-full of beets. No way to hide them before the soldiers came. "Quick, close the trap door," the Rebbe said.

Simon and Eli dragged the root cellar door into place, then quickly strew hay over it so the entrance was hidden.

Two horses, pulling an empty cart, clopped down the road to the village. Two soldiers sat astride the horses. Two others sat in the cart, their boots dangling over the edge.

"Woah!" yelled one of the riders. The horses came to a halt before the barrel. The soldiers hopped to the ground. Yossi fought not to tremble. He forced himself not to look at the glistening curved blades of the soldiers' sabers, hanging at their waists.

The soldiers advanced. "I see you have

had an excellent harvest, Jews," the tall-est one said in Russian.

"Not so good, sirs, not so good," the Rebbe answered in Russian, indicating the half-full barrel. Shuffling his feet like an old man, he kicked more straw over the root cellar door.

Please, God, don't let them see, Yossi prayed.

"Plenty enough for us, eh, Misha?" sneered another soldier. Short and round, he walked with a swagger that would have been comical, Yossi thought — if this had been a comical situation.

"And you so kindly have done all the digging for us," a skinny soldier said. His mate, a red-cheeked fellow with a thick brown moustache, joined him in a jeering laugh.

The one called Misha rested a hand on the handle of his saber. He seemed to be the leader. "Start loading — into the cart."

The Jews stood there.

"Now!"

"But sirs," the Rebbe said, "we have worked hard, planting and weeding and tending these beets. They are ours."

"Be quiet, you fool!" Misha drew out his saber and held it high. It glistened in the sunlight. Gasping, the Jews took a step back. But Yossi saw that, despite his brave words and his raised weapon, Misha did not look directly at the Rebbe. He kept his eyes to the side. Yossi wondered why.

But there was no time to wonder. "Now!" Misha roared again, as the other three soldiers pulled out their sabers. Without a word, the villagers began to load the remaining beets into the soldiers' cart.

Bitterly, Yossi dumped armful after armful into the cart. All that work, all that hope — for nothing. He longed to do something to stop the soldiers, to chase them away, to punish them. But what? He knew that if he so much as opened his mouth to protest, not only would he get killed, but worse, he would bring the wrath of the soldiers on the entire village. So he

stood there, full of fury and fear, making powerless fists.

Finally the barrel stood empty.

"Next time," Misha yelled, "no back talk, old man, or heads will roll!"

The soldiers sheathed their sabers and rode away.

All the villagers gathered around the Rebbe. Some were cursing. Many were weeping.

"Rebbe, Rebbe, they almost took your life!"

"Those thieving rogues, may God punish them!"

"What will we do? What will we do?"

"Come, come," said the Rebbe, "not a hair on my head is hurt. And at least they didn't take the beets in the root cellar. We still have almost half the crop."

"And what will we do this winter when those are gone and our stomachs are growling?" Eli said bitterly.

"We'll manage," the Rebbe said. "As we always have."

A sob rang out, and Yossi recognized Mama's cry. Papa put his arms around her and held her. Yossi saw that Miriam was crying, too.

He felt like crying himself. It was terrible to feel so powerless. But he didn't want to cry. He wanted to fight back, to teach the soldiers a lesson.

Someday he would, Yossi vowed. He'd think of something, anything, to pay the soldiers back.

Chapter Five

The Jews worked feverishly through that night and the next to gather in the harvest. Thankfully, the soldiers did not return, and the potatoes and turnips were safely hidden in the root cellar.

Now, several days later, the villagers stood in a grassy patch beside the tumble-down hut that served as Braslav's *schul*, or synagogue. Tonight was the start of

Sukkot, the week-long Jewish harvest festival, when Jews gave thanks for the blessings of the land. They were building the *sukkah*, or house of branches, that symbolized the green, bountiful earth. Morning and evening, throughout Sukkot, they would gather under the shade of the sukkah, to pray and celebrate.

First, Papa and Simon drove twelve slender poles into the ground, two rows of six facing each other. Then they attached cross pieces to make a grid.

"Now we need willow branches for the walls," Mama said. "Miriam, down you go to the stream bank and gather some. Long and leafy, mind."

Daniel sprang forward. "I'll go with her," he said. Miriam blushed. Daniel blushed. "Just to keep her safe," he added. "In case of soldiers."

"Big, brave hero," Jonah said sourly. "What could you do?"

"I'll protect her," Daniel said firmly.

"And a little time alone doesn't hurt,

either," Golda observed, and everyone laughed.

Giggling, Miriam and Daniel set off. The villagers waited. And waited.

"Where are those two?" Papa asked.

"Gathering more than willow branches, I dare say," Golda said, arching her eyebrows.

"They're taking an awfully long time," Mama said. "What if —"

But just then Miriam and Daniel came back, their arms full of branches. Behind the screen of leaves, their hands were entwined, and they gazed lovingly at each other.

"Miriam! Daniel!" Golda scolded. "Stop with the doe eyes and get those branches over here."

Everyone turned. Miriam and Daniel dropped hands and turned tomato-red. Laughter rang out. "You're not married yet, you two!" Mama said, wagging her finger.

"Such lovebirds," Sadie sighed.

Teasing the red-faced pair, the villagers began weaving the long willow branches in and out of the wooden grid, turning the two sides of the sukkah into green, leafy walls.

Yossi pressed forward, willow branch in hand. "Here, let me." He tried to squeeze his way to the front, but Jonah turned watery eyes on him. "Go away, little pest." Several people snickered. "Don't let him get near the sukkah — you know what happened to the beets," Jonah added. There was more laughter. Yossi turned away, scowling.

Once the branches had been woven into place, the villagers brought baskets of long-necked gourds, ears of corn, apples and pears, onions and herbs. All these they wove into the leaves, turning the walls into a garden paradise.

Yossi grabbed an apple and tucked its stem between two entwined branches. The stem slipped out. Yossi shoved it in again, bruising the apple. The apple fell.

Bending to pick it up, he stomped on it.

Golda had seen. "Yossi Mendelsohn, scram! You'll ruin everything."

No one lets me help, Yossi thought. How can I show what I can do if they don't give me a chance?

He began to walk away. But then the Rebbe's voice rang out, "Now for the roof. Bring the cornstalks. Let's crown our beautiful sukkah!"

Everyone gathered around as Simon stepped forward with an armful of cornstalks. The sukkah was almost done. All that remained was to lay a thicket of stalks across the top. Yossi loved this part. He loved to see the sukkah's roof take shape, throwing dappled shadows on the ground, turning the sukkah into a shady bower. Although it was only made of leaves, the sukkah felt safe and holy — shelter in a world of trouble.

Papa and Simon went to fetch a ladder.

Then Yossi got an idea.

With his stilts, he could lay the roof.

All by himself — no ladder needed. Then they'd see what a fine helper he could be!

Yossi's stilts were leaning against the side of the schul. He jumped onto them and walked back to the villagers.

"Wait!" he cried. "Let me. I can do it!" Yossi scooped the cornstalks out of Simon's arms. Hands full of stalks, he hugged the stilts to his sides. He struggled for balance. A cornstalk fell. No matter. Yossi gripped the stilts against his sides, staggered a moment, then balanced perfectly.

"Him? The klutz? Woe is us!" Jonah murmured. Several people chuckled, but others said, "No, look, he can do it," and "Good for you, Yossi."

The praise rang in Yossi's ears. Yes, he could do it. Left, right, left, right, down the center of the sukkah, between the walls. Now, all he had to do was separate one cornstalk from the rest, without letting go of the stilts ... Elbows in! ... Lay it across ... there. He'd done it. How

lovely the cornstalk looked, resting upon the two leafy walls of the sukkah.

"Good work, Yossi," the Rebbe said.

Yossi grinned but didn't dare look aside.

Next cornstalk. Stuck in the pile. Yank. Elbows in! Dusty cornstalks tickling his nose. Stagger left, right, left. Come on, you silly stalk! Tangled.

"Look at Yossi dance," Jonah jeered.

Yossi's cheeks flamed. Good thing no one could see. Too bad *he* couldn't see, either. Cornstalks in his face. Stilts slipping. Elbows in! Cornstalk up his nose. Tickle. "Ah—" Blindly stepping from side to side. "Ah —" Dried leaves scratching his cheeks. "Choooo!"

One stilt caught in one sukkah wall, the other in the opposite wall. Yossi shot forward. Up flew the cornstalks. Down came the walls. Yossi crashed onto a tangle of willow branches, onions, poles, apples and pumpkins. The cornstalks landed on his head.

"Yossi!" Mama screamed.

"The sukkah!" the Rebbe wailed.

"Lord save us!" Golda cried.

"Clumsy oaf!" Jonah said. "I told you he'd destroy the sukkah."

Yossi wished he could stay buried beneath the cornstalks. Unfortunately, Papa yanked him to his feet. Papa's face was white with rage. Mama's was red with shame.

"Go home!" Papa roared. "And take those worthless sticks with you!"

Miserably, Yossi gathered up his stilts and slunk out of the crowd. "Useless fool," he heard.

"Troublesome pest."

"Bumbling brat."

But I could have … Yossi said to himself. I would have … I meant to…

But he knew that meaning to didn't make up for anything. This time, he was really in disgrace.

Chapter Six

The Rebbe poured wine into a chipped clay goblet. "Now, my friends, let us say *Kaddish*, and thank the Lord for all the blessings He has bestowed on us."

It was that evening. Yossi stood in the sukkah — now completely rebuilt — with Mama, Papa, Miriam and the rest of the villagers. Together they were celebrating the first evening service of Sukkot.

"Give thanks to the Lord, for the Lord is good," Yossi chanted in Hebrew along with the congregation. "The Lord's kindness endures forever."

The Rebbe raised the goblet and took a sip of wine. As he lifted his arm, Yossi looked up, up to the roof of the sukkah. Through the leafy cornstalks, patches of yellow moonlight shown down on the villagers, lighting their faces with gold.

Yes, Yossi thought, the Lord *was* good. Despite Yossi's disaster, the sukkah was a place of beauty, graced with the abundance of field and garden. And even though the soldiers had taken half the beets, the root cellar still bulged with turnips and potatoes. There was food aplenty for the winter.

So, too, were Mama and Papa good. To be sure, they'd punished him severely, restricting him to the cottage for the next week. Still, they'd let him out for a few hours tonight, to attend services. And they hadn't burned his stilts. Yet.

There were many blessings to thank God for this Sukkot, Yossi reflected.

In his left hand, the Rebbe took an oval-shaped, lemon-like yellow fruit. Called an *etrog*, it symbolized the bounty of the earth. In his right hand, he took a palm branch intertwined with twigs of myrtle and willow, called a *lulav*. Chanting a prayer, the Rebbe waved the lulav up and down, turning first to the north, then to the south, east and west, to show God's presence everywhere.

Yossi watched the Rebbe turn. North, south, east, west. Everywhere in the whole wide world, there God was. And where would he — Yossi — go, if he could go anywhere? He remembered the place the villagers had spoken of. Canada. That sounded like a fine place. He didn't know exactly where it was, though he knew it was far away, across Russia, across Europe, across the Atlantic Ocean. You would have to take a ship to get there. A big ship. And he, Yossi, would sit with the captain and look out for land, the green land of Canada ...

"*Baruch atah adonoi* ...," the Rebbe began, and Yossi, awakened from his dream-voyage, joined in. "Blessed art Thou, O Lord our God ..." Like the other villagers, while praying he *davened,* swaying forward and back, forward and back, to the rhythm of the prayers. It was a comforting motion, davening, like the way Mama used to rock him when he was a baby. "... *elohainu melech ha'olom* ... king of the universe ..."

A distant sound. Thump, thump ... Closer now. Pounding. Hoof beats.

The soldiers.

Yossi's heart started pounding in rhythm. Others began to get agitated, to whisper among themselves. The Rebbe kept praying.

The hoof beats were practically upon the sukkah. Villagers exchanged terrified looks. The hoof beats stopped. Boots thudded on the ground.

The Rebbe motioned the villagers to

continue praying. They did so, though they glanced around nervously. The words stuck in Yossi's throat, but he forced them out.

"*Ah-sher kiddish-ah-nu …*"

Four soldiers — the same ones who'd stolen the beets — crowded into the sukkah. "Well, isn't this a cosy little party, eh, Yuri?" Misha said.

The short, round soldier barked a harsh laugh. "And they didn't even invite us, Misha."

The villagers kept davening, bending and swaying, chanting in low voices.

"*B'mitz-voh sav …*"

Yossi tried to keep his eyes on his prayer book but, as if they had a will of their own, they were drawn to the four soldiers. He noticed that, despite their haughty expressions, the soldiers did not look directly at the Rebbe. Like the time they stole the beets, they kept their eyes away from him. How strange, Yossi thought.

"Not very neighborly," said the soldier

with the bristly mustache. "And look at the feast hanging on the walls. We would have missed it all — and us poor souls going hungry all the time."

"I'm hungry right now," the fourth soldier said. A skinny fellow, he had a small head, and his sheepskin hat fell down over his ears.

"Hungry, Andrei, my friend?" Misha said. "In the midst of such plenty?"

"Say, Misha, you've given me an idea!" Andrei, the skinny one said, and, drawing out his saber, he hacked an apple off the sukkah wall. Shouting, the other soldiers began to pluck fruits and vegetables from the sukkah and stuff them in their mouths.

The Rebbe raised his head from his prayer book. Gazing at Misha, he said, "You are in a house of God. Show respect, or leave."

Misha seemed to flinch, but then he pulled out his saber. "A house?" he jeered. "You call this a house?" He slashed at the leaves. The wall began to lean.

Laughing, the other soldiers swiped at the walls. Pears and onions and gourds fell to the ground. The walls tilted inward. The people stood frozen, clutching their prayer books.

"You have desecrated the house of God, and He will punish you," the Rebbe intoned, pointing at each soldier in turn. Yossi noticed that each looked away, then made a swift motion with his fingers, the Russian sign of protection against the devil. Now why did they do that? Yossi wondered.

Misha shouted in a blustering voice, "God, you say? You dare to threaten me, you Jewish devil? *I* will do the punishing around here." He turned to his fellows. "Yuri, Andrei, Boris, seize their books. Now!"

The soldiers moved among the villagers, grabbing the prayer books from their hands. "No!" Eli yelled, and received a slap across the face. Daniel tried to hold onto his prayer book, but a blow sent him to the ground. Wails and cries went up.

"Worthless books, full of Jewish mumbo-jumbo, eh, friends?" Misha said. He laughed, but Yossi could tell it was a forced laugh, full of false courage.

"Hebrew hocus-pocus," Yuri agreed.

When all the prayer books had been gathered, the soldiers flung them to the ground. Boris struck a match. With a crackle, the books ignited. Yossi saw pages twist as if in agony before they surrendered to the flames.

Some villagers screamed. Others wept. Only the Rebbe looked straight ahead, still chanting the Sukkot prayers.

"Let that be a lesson to you, Jews," Misha growled. "*We* make the rules around here. *We* do the punishing. Not your God who sends down his word in stupid backward writing!"

The flames blazed higher. The soldiers laughed, but at the same time they drew back, as if shrinking from more than just the heat of the fire.

Odd, Yossi thought.

But he had no time to figure it out, for the walls began to fall in. Shrieking, the villagers fled. The soldiers leaped to their horses and galloped away. The sukkah collapsed in an inferno of flame and ash. The people huddled together beside the ruins, weeping.

"Curse them!" Eli said.

"May God strike them dead!" yelled Simon.

"Such a sin, to burn the holy books," Golda moaned.

"Oh, Rebbe, Rebbe, what will we do?" Sadie said, wiping her eyes.

"We must leave," Rivka said.

"Yes, we must," Simon agreed. "But how? And where could we go?"

"Come, come, everyone," the Rebbe said. Everyone drew closer. "I have news."

"News? What news?" Golda said, squirming to the front.

"Hush, Golda, let the Rebbe talk, and

then you'll hear what news," Sadie scolded.

"The Rebbe of Vladstok sent me a secret message," the Rebbe said. "Many of his villagers have escaped to Canada. And there are people over there, he says, good people, who will help us emigrate to Canada, if only we can get away from Braslav."

"Canada," Yossi whispered. Just like in his daydream!

"That's never, then," Eli said gloomily.

"Hush, Eli, don't say that," Mama said.

"Well, how are we to get away, I ask you?" Eli returned. "The soldiers watch us like hawks. Do you think they'll just stand aside and say, 'Very well, Jews of Braslav, off you go, have a nice trip'? I tell you, it's impossible."

"Nothing is impossible, with God's help," the Rebbe said. "If the soldiers could be distracted somehow, if their attention could be diverted from Braslav, even for just an hour, we could get away. We only have to get to Vladstok, after all. It's just across the river."

Simon nodded. "The Rebbe's right. From there, people will shelter us from village to village, until we reach the sea."

"We must be ready to go at a moment's notice," the Rebbe said. "Pack a bag, each family. A small bag, mind, for we may be many days on foot. Take only what you can carry. Who knows? Perhaps a chance will come sooner than we think."

Yossi listened with excitement. If only he could find a way to distract the soldiers. He'd save the village. Then people would be proud of him. They'd stop laughing at him. They'd forget how he'd wrecked the sukkah, and dropped the beets, and all the other things he'd done wrong.

Without thinking, he blurted, "I'll do it!"

"Do what, Yossele?" Papa asked, looking at him.

"Find a way to distract the soldiers, so we can get away."

"Hah!" everyone scoffed, Jonah loudest of all.

"You!"

"Spindle-legs!"

"The long-legged hero!"

For once, Yossi ignored them. He paid no attention to their jeers. To be sure, he had no idea what had prompted him to speak out. Nor did he have the slightest notion how he would do what he'd promised. But he was determined to find a way. To prove that he was a hero — and not a fool.

Chapter Seven

The cottage was quiet. The village was silent. All were asleep.

All except Yossi. Bathed in yellow moonlight, he lay wide-eyed on his bed, remembering. The fear on the faces of his neighbors … the pages of the prayer books curling, smoldering … the grim determination in the Rebbe's eyes … the strange sideways glances of the soldiers …

Yossi wondered about that. The soldiers were ten times stronger than the villagers — no, a hundred times — yet they'd been uneasy. They'd refused to look the Rebbe in the face, and they'd made that funny hand sign, to ward off the devil. They'd seemed to shrink back from the burning books which they themselves had thrown onto the fire. It didn't make sense, unless …

Yossi sat upright. Unless they were afraid! But afraid of what? The Jews? The Rebbe? The funny Hebrew writing and the strange-sounding prayers?

Ridiculous. The soldiers knew how weak and defenseless the Jews were. That was why they bullied them all the time. And yet, Yossi was sure, they feared something. Not the Jews' might, surely, but something else. Something deeper. It was as if they feared that the Jews held some kind of power over them, some force of enchantment.

A tingle went up Yossi's back. So the

soldiers were not all-powerful. In spite of their brave words and their bold deeds, they had a weakness. And maybe he, Yossi, could find out what that weakness was and use it to scare them even more — scare them off long enough to let the people of Braslav escape. Then he'd fulfill the vow he'd made … and be a hero!

But first, he had to find out more. He had to figure out how to give the soldiers the fright of their lives.

And that meant he had to spy on them.

Yossi listened. Papa was snoring gently. Mama and Miriam were breathing softly. Yossi knew Mama and Papa would kill him if they found out. They'd give him so many punishments, he'd be serving them until his beard turned gray.

But he had to go. He had to find a way.

Scarcely breathing, he slipped out of bed, tiptoed across the cottage, past the traveling case that lay packed and ready — "Who knows?" Papa had said with a shrug earlier that evening; "Maybe a miracle will happen" — and unlatched the door. The latch groaned. Yossi held his breath. Papa rolled over. Mama sighed. Yossi crept outside and pulled the door shut. Then he ran.

Five nights later, Yossi crouched in his usual hiding place behind a stout fir tree. It was all he could do not to stamp with frustration.

For four nights he had spied on the soldiers. For four nights he had snuck out of the cottage, risking discovery and punishment. For four nights he had watched and listened.

And for four nights, he'd heard nothing.

Oh, he'd heard plenty of complaints. The soldiers seemed to do nothing but complain. Their boots pinched. Their greatcoats were wearing thin. Their sabers were old. Their huts were falling down.

But so far he'd heard nothing useful. Nothing that would help him.

And he was beginning to wonder if it

had been a stupid idea after all, to think that he could find out what they were afraid of, and turn it against them. To help the Jews escape.

Now, on the fifth night, he promised himself he'd try one last time. If he didn't learn anything tonight, he'd give up.

In the flickering firelight, Misha took a long drink from a bottle, wiped his mouth with his sleeve and handed the bottle to Andrei, the skinny one, sitting on the ground next to him.

"I'm hungry," Andrei said.

"Me, too," said Boris, the fellow with the bristly mustache.

"Who wouldn't be, with the miserable rations the army gives us?" Misha grumbled.

More complaints, Yossi thought. For a change.

Yuri, the chubby soldier, took a gulp. "A crust of black bread, a handful of buckwheat groats, a lump of hard cheese … Pitiful!"

"Any more of the Jews' beets left?" Misha asked.

At the word "Jews," Yossi's ears pricked up.

"All gone," Boris said with a sigh.

"Already?" Misha said. "Ah, they were good while they lasted."

Yuri chuckled. "Especially since we didn't have to do the digging."

Andrei grinned. "Just plucked them out of the barrel."

"Speaking of plucking," Misha boasted, "how about that raid the other night, when we plucked the food off the walls of that crazy shelter, eh?"

Boris barked out a laugh. "A whole meal laid out in front of us. Very kind of the Jews."

Andrei drank. "Why'd they hang the fruit on the walls, anyway?"

"Some stupid Jewish custom," Misha said.

Boris took a long swallow, then slapped his knee. "Hey, fellows, did you see their faces when we took the prayer books?"

Yuri spat. "Can't read that backward writing anyway."

"That's what the Jews are — backward," Misha said. He wagged his head like a simpleton, and the others roared with laughter.

"No wonder the Czar wants to get rid of the devils," Andrei said.

"Devils is right," Yuri agreed. "They're sons of the evil one, and no mistake."

The laughter died away and a shiver seemed to run through the group. Then Misha said in a low voice, "And that leader, the priest, what d'you call him, ooh, I didn't like the look in his eyes."

Andrei huddled forward. "It's as if he knows something ... as if he could cast a spell ..."

They *are* afraid! Yossi thought. Afraid of the Rebbe!

Boris shook his head. "I don't like this talk of spells. Reminds me of the tales my granny used to tell, of witches and goblins."

Andrei leaned forward and whispered, "Baba Yaga ..."

"Don't say that name!" Misha shouted.

"Oh, my aunties had my hair standing on end with tales of that crone, I can tell you," Yuri said.

Misha drank, then looked around the circle. "Who wouldn't be scared of Baba Yaga? The most powerful witch in the forest."

"Her hut — my granny swore this was true — sits on chicken feet," Boris said. "And Baba Yaga can make it turn in any direction, so you can never hide from her."

"I've heard her fence is built of human bones," Andrei added.

"With hollow-eyed skulls perched on the fence posts, lit by a ghostly fire," Yuri put in.

With a shudder, all four soldiers drew closer together around the fire.

Yossi watched with growing interest. So he'd been right. The soldiers were

scared. Superstitious. Big, brave fellows! They thought the Rebbe could put a spell on them. And they were even more afraid of Baba Yaga. Yossi had heard of the famous Russian witch. Jews didn't believe in her, nor in the devil and demon tales their Russian neighbors told. But the soldiers were terrified of her!

Andrei took a long sip. "They say she's tall and skinny, with long, long legs."

Yuri nodded. "Baba Yaga Bony Legs, I've heard her called."

"Skinny as a skeleton ..."

"Long, stringy hair ..."

"Razor-sharp fingernails ..."

"And that flying mortar she travels in — she can go anywhere she pleases, just by saying the magic word," Misha put in, his face pinched with fear.

"While with her broomstick, she brushes away her tracks," Andrei added.

Boris looked over his shoulder. "She could be flying through the forest right now!"

A shiver seemed to go through the entire group. "Hush!" Misha ordered.

Yuri squirmed. "My granny says Baba Yaga eats little children, whole."

"Not just children. Grown men, too," Andrei said.

"Don't say that!" Misha cried.

"Yet she never gets fat, no matter how much she eats," Yuri said.

Misha nodded. "That's why she has to keep catching more and more victims."

Boris drank. "Her appetite's never satisfied."

Yuri shuddered. "God preserve me from such unnatural cravings, but Baba Yaga's not the only one who's hungry all the time. I'm ravenous!"

Misha nodded in agreement. "I can feel my poor empty belly rubbing against my backbone."

Andrei sighed. "Ah, what I would give for a fire-roasted potato right now."

"Forget it, Andrei, we have no potatoes," Boris said.

"But the Jews do," Yuri remembered.

"True, but they're all harvested," Boris returned. "Last time we rode into the village, the fields were empty."

"So what? I think I know where they store the crops," Misha said.

"You do? Where?"

"In a root cellar, by the garden. Remember when we took the beets? They kept kicking straw around a certain spot, as if they didn't want us to see …"

"But *you* saw, Misha, you sly rascal," Andrei said admiringly.

Grinning, Misha gave a mock bow.

"Think of all those potatoes, just sitting there," Yuri said.

"Potato stew … Fried potatoes … Potato dumplings …"

All four gazed dreamily into the fire. Then Misha sat up straight. "Let's go get them!"

"What, tonight?" Andrei said.

"Yes, tonight. I'm starving," Misha said.

"What better time, with the Jews all asleep?" Yuri laughed.

"Great idea!" Boris said. "Come, we'll saddle the horses —"

Misha shook his head. "But no galloping into the village. Let's keep it quiet. We'll walk the horses. It'll be more of a joke that way — and we love a good joke, don't we, friends?"

"Especially on the Jews!" Yuri added, and the others shouted their agreement.

Misha glanced at the sky. "The moon'll set in an hour or two. We'll wait until full dark, then sneak into the village. They'll hear nothing. See nothing. What a surprise in the morning, when they find their precious potatoes gone!"

"And if they wake up?" Yuri said.

In answer, Misha thrust a stick into the fire, then held its burning tip aloft. "Then we burn them out."

"Either way, we still get the potatoes," Andrei said gleefully. "What a feast we'll have."

"Don't torture me," Yuri said. "I can't wait!"

Neither could he! Yossi told himself. The soldiers would be on the road in a matter of hours. He had to warn the villagers, so they could protect the root cellar. If they lost the potatoes, as well as the beets, there wouldn't be enough food for winter. But how could the Jews fend off the soldiers? What were unarmed villagers against soldiers with sabers?

Still, the Jews couldn't simply stand by and see their food stolen. If only they could —

Wait.

An idea came into Yossi's head. A brilliant idea. A way to scare off the soldiers. Give them the fright of their lives.

And, if it worked, it would give the Jews a chance to escape.

Chapter Eight

Panting, Yossi let himself into the cottage. Dear God, what was he going to do? There was so little time. Within two hours — less than that, now — he had to prepare to carry out his plan, and get himself into place, and warn the Jews to get ready to run, and —

Two eyes shone at him in the dark. Miriam!

For a moment, Yossi was terrified, thinking he'd been caught. But then he was flooded with relief. Miriam would help him. With her assistance, he could get ready in time. And she could help him rouse the people.

Yossi beckoned to his sister. Silently she followed him outside. In a low voice, he told her what the soldiers were planning to do.

"Yossi!" she whispered in alarm. "We'll lose our food — or our homes!"

"No, Miriam," he said. "I have a plan."

Miriam listened carefully. Then she shook her head. "Yossi, it's madness! What if it doesn't work? They'll kill you!"

Yossi knew that was true. But what else could he do? What else could any of them do? It was worth a try. It was better than starving — or being burned out.

"It *will* work," he insisted. "Only help me get ready."

Silently he and Miriam tiptoed around the village. They gathered Mama's string mop, Rivka's head scarf, a long black cloth hanging on Golda's clothesline, several pairs of Sadie's knitting needles, Simon's broom, a small clay lantern from Eli's pottery workshop and, last of all, Yossi's stilts.

"Now," Yossi whispered, "go wake everybody up and tell them to get ready. Tell them to gather their bags and meet on the other side of the village, away from the garden, by the road to Vladstok."

"But Yossi," Miriam said, "how will I make them do it? I can't tell them what you're planning. If they think this is your idea, they'll never follow me."

She was right, Yossi realized. Clumsy Yossi. Bumbling Yossi. Of course the villagers wouldn't trust a plan *he* had hatched. He gazed into the darkness, almost fancying he heard footsteps already. "Tell them ... tell them ..." Think! "Tell them the soldiers are planning to burn down the village — that's true enough — and that we may have a chance to escape in the confusion. A good chance — but only if everyone is ready."

"Right." Miriam nodded. "And if they ask how I know, I'll say … I'll say I overheard them talking during the raid the other night. And I'll tell Mama and Papa that you are helping the others get ready."

"Good thinking, Miriam," Yossi said. "Now, hurry!"

Miriam hugged her brother. Then she ran off into the darkness.

Yossi yanked the string mop off its handle. He stuck the mop on his head, letting the long stringy ropes hang over his face, then tied on the head scarf to hold it in place. He wrapped the black cloth round and round himself, letting it dangle over his feet. He fastened the knitting needles to the backs of his hands with string, so their points jutted out beyond his fingers. He overturned the clay lantern onto the broomstick. Finally, he hopped up onto his stilts and marched to the root cellar.

Behind him, Yossi heard drunken whispers and slow hoof beats. A baby cried and was hushed. A lantern flared, then was extinguished. Dark shapes moved in the shadows.

They had listened to Miriam, he thought with relief, willing them to hurry, hurry.

The moon began to set. It slanted low in the sky behind Yossi, casting his shadow on the ground before him. In the shadowy shape, Yossi saw a tall, skinny creature towering on long, bony legs. Her stringy hair hung down past her shoulders, her sharp fingernails pierced the night air, and a human skull sat atop her broomstick, moonlight glinting through its empty eye sockets.

The last glimmer of moonlight faded. Drunken whispers floated down the road from the soldiers' encampment.

Yossi moved behind a spreading birch tree. His heart pounding, he waited.

Chapter Nine

"Where're those potatoes? Let me at 'em," Boris said drunkenly.

"Hush, you fool!" That was Misha's voice. "We don't want the Jews to know we're here. We want it to be a surprise, remember?"

"Oh, I wish I could see their faces when they find the potatoes gone," Andrei said.

"You'll be too busy stuffing your own

face," Yuri said with a guffaw.

Yossi stayed behind the tree, waiting for the right moment. He couldn't let the soldiers get a good look at him. He had to take them completely by surprise.

"Where's that darn root cellar, anyway?" Yuri slurred. "You said you knew where it was, Misha."

"Shut your mouth!" Misha rasped. "It must be around here somewhere. Where else could it be? Look for straw. Is that straw there …?"

There were stumbling footsteps for several moments, then the sound of a collision. "Watch where you're going!" Andrei said.

"You blundered into me, you oaf!" Boris returned.

"Shut up, both of you," Misha snapped. "Now, get out of my way — ooofff!" There was a sprawling sound. Then, "Here it is! I've found the trap door."

"Where? Where?" Yuri said.

"We'll soon have a feast, friends," Boris said.

"I don't see anything," Andrei said.

"Blasted door," Misha said. "Help me, it's stuck."

There was a scuffling sound as all four soldiers flopped to the ground.

"Where?"

"Is that the handle?"

"No, that's my foot, you fool!"

Now, Yossi thought.

He stepped out from the shadows. Pitching his voice high, he screeched, "What's this, my lovely lads? Fattening yourselves up for me, are you?"

Four heads looked up. Four mouths fell open.

Baba Yaga stalked closer. She waved one long-nailed hand. "Ooohh, four tasty fellows. What luck! I'm simply ravenous!"

"Whaa —"

"Holy mother of God —"

"It can't be —"

"What a delicious meal you boys will make, roasted slow and crisp in my oven, turned on the spit to perfection. I can

hardly wait to taste the first bite. Who will I eat first, I wonder? Will it be you? Or you? Or you? Or you?" She pointed a razor-sharp finger at each soldier in turn.

The soldiers scrambled to their feet, knocking over one another in their haste.

"It's her —"

"The witch —"

"Baba Yaga!"

Baba Yaga cackled, tossing her stringy hair as she stalked closer. "Yes, it is I, come to snare you for my pot." She hefted the skull on the end of her broomstick. "And your skulls, once I've picked them clean, will make handsome additions to my collection — just like this one."

The soldiers began to back up, but Baba Yaga advanced just as quickly. Her long fingernails glittered. The skull rattled on the broomstick. Perched on her long bony legs, she towered over the cringing soldiers. "My belly is empty. My appetite is gnawing. My mouth is watering. I want to eat you — NOW!"

The soldiers hesitated no longer. Shrieking, they ran for their lives.

"Save me!"

"Help!"

"Yikes!"

"Whaaa —"

The soldiers disappeared down the road, back towards their encampment. Spooked, their horses had already disappeared.

Yossi waited until they were completely out of sight, until he could no longer hear footsteps. He threw back his head and laughed. Then, as quickly as he could, he hopped down from his stilts, tore off the mop and scarf and cloth, threw down the broomstick and lantern, scattered the knitting needles. Tucking his stilts under his arm, he ran in the opposite direction.

The villagers were crouching in the shadows cast by the ruins of the sukkah. Mama tore herself from the crowd. "Yossi! Oh, my Yossele, where were you? I was so scared —"

"I'm fine, Mama, don't worry."

Everyone pressed close. "Did it work, Yossi?" Miriam said. "Are they gone?"

"Gone, Miriam! Running for their lives!"

"You chased the soldiers off, Yossi?" the Rebbe said, hardly daring to believe it.

"You?" Golda repeated.

"*You*?" Jonah echoed.

Yossi enjoyed their surprise. "Yes, I."

Mama grabbed him, holding him close. "Yossi, what were you thinking? You could have been killed —"

The Rebbe interrupted, "Far away, Yossi? Did you chase them far?"

Yossi shook free of Mama. At the rate the soldiers were running, he didn't think they'd stop for a long time. He grinned. "Far, far away."

"But how, Yossi?" Sadie said. "How did you do it?"

Yossi looked around. All the people were looking at him with wonderment. With awe. With respect. He had said he would do it, and he had. Finally, the people believed him. This was the moment he had waited for. He smiled mischievously. "Oh … I just used my stilts."

"His stilts!" Golda cried. "I always knew those stilts would come in handy. If I said it once, I said it a thousand times: 'Yossi Mendelsohn, he's so clever with those stilts!' I knew it in my bones, friends."

The Rebbe put up his hand. "Enough, Golda." He turned to Yossi, pride and puzzlement mixed on his face. "My boy, I don't know how you did it — and I don't I think I want to know," he added with a twinkle, "but I fear we have misjudged you. Somehow you, a mere lad, outwitted the soldiers. Like David, who slew Goliath, with cunning — and a little help from God — you have saved us, Yossele."

Yossi felt a hand squeeze his shoulder. He looked up into Papa's smiling eyes. He looked around at all the faces. Some people's eyes were filled with tears. Others were smiling. All were looking at him as if he were a hero. Even Jonah. Even those who had laughed at him and mocked him.

Yossi grinned, basking in the admiration. How sweet it was! No more clumsy Yossi. No more stupid Yossi.

"But this is no time for praise," the Rebbe went on. "There's not a moment to lose. Now is our chance. Grab your bags, my friends, and let's be off — to freedom!"

The villagers of Braslav hurried down the road to Vladstok, led by a young boy with two long sticks tucked under his arm.

Chapter Ten

Weeks later, Yossi stood on the deck of an enormous ship. Wind whipped his face, and he had to hold onto his cloth cap with both hands to keep it from flying overboard.

Yossi scanned from side to side. Maybe today, the sailors had said. But all Yossi could see were waves, endless curls of gray-green waves, and now sooty-looking gulls with long black beaks. Lord, he was weary of the endless water!

Still, it was better than the alternative. Better than remaining in Braslav.

It had been a long, hard journey to the sea. Hiding by day, tramping through woods by night, always fearful, always hungry, grateful for the shelter given by Jews in small villages along the way. Once they'd huddled in a coal cellar while soldiers' boots had thundered on the wooden planks overhead. Another time they'd hidden in a hayloft while soldiers had burned the village to the ground. Afterward, the survivors had joined their ranks. Week after week, through rain squalls and snowstorms, village by village, hiding place to hiding place, they'd made their way across Russia, through Austria, across Germany, by boat to England where, with the last of their money, they'd booked passage on a steamship bound for Canada.

Canada. Yossi turned the name over and over in his mind. It had enormous forests, he'd heard, and great rushing rivers, and mountains so high that snow never melted from their summits. It sounded like a beautiful, abundant land. Best of all, it had no soldiers to force the people into misery and starvation. In Canada, he'd heard, you could be a Jew, and chant the prayers, and celebrate the holidays, and no one hated you for it, or wanted to harm you or kill you. That was the most wonderful thing of all.

Yossi scanned the horizon. Waves, nothing but waves. When would they ever — Wait. Was that ...? That distant speck ... That darker smudge where the water met the sky ... Could it be ...? Were his eyes fooling him, or was that really —

"Rebbe!" Yossi yelled. "I see land! I see Canada!"

All the villagers rushed up onto deck.

"Where?"

"There?"

"I don't see anything."

"There! Look!"

"Trees!"

"Ships!"

"Canada!"

A joyful cry went up from the crowd, mingled with tears and laughter. Yossi felt a tightness in his throat.

Then he was surprised to feel a hand on his shoulder. He turned, to see a mysterious smile on the Rebbe's face. "Rebbe … what …?"

"Yossi, before we land, there is something I must say. Something I must do, for all the people of Braslav," the Rebbe began.

Yossi looked around. All the villagers had gathered 'round. Everyone's eyes were twinkling. Even Mama's and Papa's and Miriam's. What was going on?

"Yossi," the Rebbe went on, "we left Braslav in such a hurry, we never properly thanked you. But we are more grateful than we can say. For your quick thinking. For your courage."

"For your steady balance!" Daniel cried,

and everyone laughed, for all now knew the tale of how Yossi had scared the soldiers away.

The Rebbe laughed along. "That, too, Yossi. But most of all, for your faith that something could be done, when most of us had given up."

Yossi felt his cheeks burning — but not with shame, for once. With pride.

The Rebbe reached into his pocket and pulled out a blue cloth bag. "On behalf of all the people of Braslav, Yossi, we want you to have this. A small token of our thanks."

The Rebbe overturned the bag and shook it. Something small and glittering fell into the palm of his hand.

The Rebbe unclasped a gold chain and fastened it around Yossi's neck. A six-sided Star of David nestled against his throat.

"Hooray for Yossi!" the people shouted. "Hooray for our hero!"

Yossi flushed with pride. Grinning, he

reached up and grasped the star in his hand. It seemed to give off a warmth of its own. Then he turned to face the green Canadian shore. He stretched out his other arm. "To our new life — in Canada."

Chapter Eleven

Jesse blinked, once, twice. His head felt
heavy, his brain murky. Colors swirled
before him; first the gray-green of ocean
waves, then shiny gold, then a deep forest green. Faces came and went: the kind
face of a bearded man in a long black
robe, and the smiling face of a girl who
looked strangely like himself, and a pair
of watery-looking eyes, and the evil leer

of a crone with a long pointed nose and sharp teeth ...

Where was he? One moment he seemed to be in a small, cramped hut, then he seemed to be on the heaving deck of a vast ship, and then he recognized the sloping eaves of his own attic ...

Jesse realized his hand was fisted at his throat. He opened his fist. Something fell against his chest.

The star. The Jewish star. Yossi's star.

Jesse looked around, puzzled. There was the bookshelf with the toppled books. There was the box with his baby clothes. There was the carton of worn ice skates. And there, on his lap, was Yossi's box.

Yes, he was definitely back in his attic. But how ...? Why ...?

Jesse shook his head as if to clear it. Had it all been a dream or had it really happened? No, it was too real to be a dream — the people, the village, the danger. He'd been there, smelled the hay and apples, seen the golden moon in Braslav's sky.

He'd *become* Yossi. Somehow he'd gone back in time and lived Yossi's life. Now he was Jesse again. How had it happened?

The star. It all had something to do with the star. The strange warmth, the feeling of going back in time. Yet now, though the star still hung around his neck, he felt perfectly normal. Yet different, too. As if, by becoming Yossi, he'd somehow become more himself. It didn't make sense. But that was all right. He felt great. What a neat feeling, to have been his great-great-grandfather for a while!

With new eagerness, Jesse examined the picture. Sure enough, that was Yossi at the front, the boy with the big grin and the same dark eyes as his own. And that pair right behind Yossi, gazing into one another's eyes, the girl dimpled and shy-looking, were Miriam and Daniel. And the woman with the care-worn face, standing beside the proud-looking man in a shabby overcoat: Mama and Papa. There was the solemn-faced Rebbe, and that chubby woman with the silly-looking hat was, of course, Golda.

Jesse's eyes roved over the picture, picking out Simon and Rivka and Sadie ... and Eli, looking as glum and sour upon reaching the shores of Canada as he had back home in Braslav.

Looking from face to face, Jesse felt a strange warmth. He knew these people — knew them like friends. Like family. They *were* family — his family. He'd never felt this way before about his ancestors. Never really thought about them at all. They were dead and gone, so who cared? But now — to his surprise — he did care. He felt close to them. To Yossi, most of all, and to Miriam, and Mama and Papa. Even to Golda, that old busybody!

Jesse scanned the faces. They looked exhausted. And no wonder, after all they'd been through. But they looked hopeful, too. And proud. Darn right! Jesse thought. They'd been brave. They'd had guts — Yossi most of all.

What a cool guy — and my very own

great-great-grandfather! Jesse thought with pride. Who would have imagined that a kid — a clumsy kid, a bumbling kid, a kid dressed up in a raggedy witch costume — could frighten off a bunch of grown soldiers? Remembering the looks on the soldiers' faces, Jesse laughed out loud.

But then he shivered. If Yossi hadn't managed to scare the soldiers away, the whole family might have died of starvation or fire — and then he, Jesse, would never have been born. That was something to be grateful for!

But not only that. He was grateful to Yossi, too, for helping the family get to Canada — to a place where people didn't hate you or kill you just because you were different. He'd never thought about it before. But now he knew how lucky he was. And not just him. His parents and grandparents and all their relatives — all because of Yossi.

"My great-great-grandfather, Yossi Mendelsohn, was a hero ...," Jesse imagined starting his report. Then he laughed. Now his problem wasn't gathering enough information — it was figuring out what to do with all the information he had! Just wait till Ms. Brannigan read his paper. She'd be blown away. So would the other kids, when he told them about Yossi. And so would Mom. She'd be thrilled to hear what he'd found out about the family.

Jesse replaced the photograph in the box. He started to take off the Jewish star, but then he stopped. No, he would leave it on. It was part of him now. "Right, Yossi?" he whispered with the faintest breath.

Tucking the box under his arm, Jesse climbed down the ladder, the golden star glittering at his neck. As he pulled the trap door shut, he almost thought he heard Yossi whisper, "Right!"

Historical Background to Jesse's Star

Jews are people who practice an ancient religion called Judaism. In effect, the people and their religion are one and the same thing.

Judaism was founded in about 2000 BC by the patriarch Abraham in the land that is now called Israel.

Throughout their history, Jews have been conquered by many other civilizations, including the Egyptians, Assyrians, Babylonians and Romans. Whoever their rulers, the Jews managed to adapt to new customs, while clinging to their religion and beliefs.

The Jews were exiled from Israel by the Romans in 135 AD, after they were defeated in a three-year war. This expulsion is known as the Diaspora, a Greek word meaning "a scattering," and the Jews were indeed scattered throughout all the countries of the Middle East and Europe.

Wherever they settled, they built centres of learning, and became known as scholars and merchants. Yet often they faced persecution and oppression. Thousands of Jews were killed in the Spanish Inquisition, and sometimes they were banished from one country after another.

Russia was one of the countries where Jews settled in the Diaspora. For more than two hundred years, periods of tolerance and acceptance of Jews alternated with periods of poverty and oppression. In 1881, following the assassination of Czar Alexander II, the persecution became more intense than ever before.

Restrictive laws ordered Jews out of their homes and villages, and a wave of pogroms swept through Russia and Eastern Europe. Soldiers and citizens attacked Jewish communities, destroyed schools and synagogues, and killed men, women and children.

As the pogroms continued, tens of thousands of refugees poured over the Russian border. Often, they were sent from country to country, as each state refused to accept them. Fortunately, immigrant resettlement organizations in the United States and Canada helped thousands of Jews immigrate to North America.

Before 1880, the Jewish population of Canada was 1,200. By 1882, it had doubled. By 1914, it had reached 120,800.

The Star of David mentioned in the story is a symbol commonly associated with Judaism, although it appears in other Middle Eastern and African cultures. Also called the Shield of David, it is supposed to represent the shape of the biblical King David's shield. The Star is made of two interlocking triangles, one pointing up and the other pointing down.

Today, the Star of David appears on the flag of Israel, and many Jewish people wear it on a necklace to proclaim their faith and their identity.